Abracadabra!

Presto!

Magic Treasure!

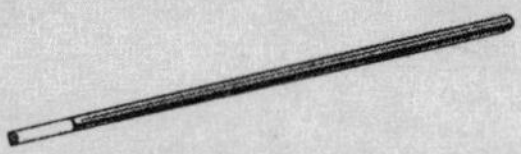

Anything can happen when you wave your magic wand!

Join the Abracadabra Club in all their Magical Mysteries.

#1: **POOF!** Rabbits Everywhere!
#2: **BOO!** Ghosts in the School!
#3: **PRESTO!** Magic Treasure!

Abracadabra!

PRESTO!
Magic Treasure!

By Peter Lerangis
Illustrated by Jim Talbot

A
LITTLE APPLE
PAPERBACK

SCHOLASTIC INC.
New York Toronto London Auckland Sydney
Mexico City New Delhi Hong Kong Buenos Aires

ISBN 0-439-22232-X

12 11 10 9 8 7 6 5 4 3 2 1 2 3 4 5 6 7/0

Printed in the U.S.A.
First Scholastic printing, January 2002

This book is dedicated to the memory of my beloved friend,
Dr. Herbert S. Strean,
who in his life spread magic wherever he went.

Contents

Abracadabra!

PRESTO!

Magic Treasure!

1

We're Not in Rebus Anymore . . .

Andrew Flingus peeked over the bus driver's shoulder. He looked at the number of miles the bus had gone. "One hundred and seven miles!" Andrew shouted. Then he burped.

Andrew had burped 107 times that day, once for each mile.

"We're here!" shouted Jessica Frimmel, looking out the bus window.

"Finally," Selena Cruz grumbled.

The bus bounced down a mountain road, past a big sign:

FROST VILLAGE "THE GREAT OUTDOORS, AT YOUR DOORSTEP!"⇨ ☆☆☆WELCOME, REBUS ELEMENTARY SCHOOL FOURTH GRADE!☆☆☆

Each year, the Rebus fourth graders took a long weekend trip. But they had never before gone to Frost Village. It was in the woods of New Hampshire, 107 burps away from Rebus, Massachusetts. And that was too far for Selena.

Selena did not like bus trips. She did not like the woods. To her, the Great Outdoors meant Too Much Sweat and Too Much Dirt.

"ATTENTION, ALL RIDERS!" shouted

Max Bleeker, whooshing a black cape and waving a magic wand. "I SHALL NOW CAUSE THIS BUS TO STOP, WITH A MAGIC SMELL! ALLAKAZOOT . . . STOPPO!"

"It's magic *spell*!" whispered Jessica. "Not *smell.*"

Max wore a black cape and top hat every single day. He truly believed he was a wizard.

Max also mixed up his words when he was nervous.

The bus slowed down, then stopped. Max was in shock. "Hey, I did it!"

Quincy Norton groaned. "The bus driver did it, Max. We are in the parking lot."

All the kids began rushing toward the door. Quincy put away his notepad. He had just finished drawing a road map of the trip. Drawing maps was one of Quincy's favorite things to do. So were reading, writing, and solving mysteries. But most of all, Quincy loved magic.

He was crazy, nutty, and wild about magic — just like Max. And Jessica. And Selena. They were the first and original four members of the Abracadabra Club, Rebus Elementary School's first magic club. Over the last few weeks, more kids had joined the club — but they weren't really in the group yet.

Mr. Beamish, the head of the Abracadabra Club, was helping kids off the bus. He had a jolly face, a small black beard, and a round head like a crystal ball. "Please, one at a time," he said.

"I can't wait to go hiking!" Jessica shouted as she climbed out.

"And finding elves and trolls and stuff!" said Max Bleeker.

"And mapping trails in the woods!" added Quincy Norton.

"And stepping in moose poo!" shouted Andrew Flingus. He jumped off the top step of the bus and landed in a mud puddle. "HAR! HAR! HAR!"

Selena froze on the bus stairs. "*Moose?* C-can't I just go home?"

Mr. Beamish took her arm and led her out of the bus. "You'll like this place, Selena. The owner is an old friend of mine. Victor Vorpal. He's a magician, too."

"Is he as good as you are?" Max asked.

"*Good? I taught him everything he knows!*" a strange voice called out.

Suddenly, from a large log cabin came a flash of light and a puff of smoke.

2

Missing Person

Out of the smoke walked a thin man. He had steel-gray eyes and a long white beard like cotton candy. As he smiled, the ends of his mustache curled upward. "Not a bad trick, eh?" he said with a giggle. "Greetings, everyone! Welcome to the Frost Village Nature Weekend."

"Boys and girls, meet Mr. Vorpal," said

Mr. Beamish. "The truth is, I taught *him* everything *he* knows."

"Oh? Well then, top this, Beamish!" Mr. Vorpal threw out his arms. From his left sleeve, a white dove suddenly flew out. He grinned. "Now, grab your bags and follow me, kids. We will drop everything off in our rooms, then meet in the lodge."

"He is cool," said Max.

"Can you do something like that, Mr. Beamish?" asked Quincy.

"In due time," Mr. Beamish said with a smile. "In due time."

He took a suitcase from the bottom of the bus and gave it to Selena. It was huge.

"What's in there, a hippopotamus?" asked Jessica.

"Nine shirts — four for indoors, four for outdoors, and one spare," said Selena. "Also nine pairs of pants, two raincoats, three jackets, long underwear, some hats, five pairs of shoes, spare boots, two dresses, and all my hairbrushes."

"We're only here for three days," said Quincy.

"You wouldn't understand," said Selena, lugging her suitcase toward the lodge.

Mr. Beamish was behind her. He was rolling a wooden trunk, bigger than Selena's suitcase. It had a curved top, metal edges, and faded stickers all over it.

The group passed through a porch made of tied-together antlers. Inside the lodge, the ceiling rose three stories high. A moose head stared out from over a huge fireplace. *Everything* was made from old tree trunks and branches — the walls, the chairs, the tables, the front desk.

Mr. Beamish and the other teachers led the kids down a long hallway. Selena and Jessica were staying together in Room 11. Jessica dropped off her bag and ran back to the lodge. Selena decided to unpack. By the time she got to the lodge, everyone was gathered around the fireplace. And Mr. Vorpal had already begun speaking.

". . . And so, Frost Village dates back to sixteen-twenty, when my ancestor, Velma Vorpal, sailed here on the good ship *Juneflower.*"

Quincy raised his hand. "Don't you mean the *Mayflower*?"

"No, she missed that boat and sailed the next month," said Mr. Vorpal sadly. "She was a great magician, but she often forgot things. After arriving in America, she got lost on the way to Plymouth Rock. That's how she ended up in Frost Village. Anyway, she put on magic shows here at the lodge. Some said she was a real wizard. Her magic collection was famous around the world. She had tricks no one could solve — and amazing costumes made of the finest material on Earth."

Jessica raised her hand. "What happened to all of her things?"

Mr. Vorpal shook his head. "No one knows. Stolen, maybe. Or lost. Velma often lost things. She was very rich, but she kept her fortune in a trunk. For safety, she buried it in the woods. She even made a map, so she wouldn't forget where it was. But she lost that, too."

A lost fortune. Selena looked out the window. Somewhere out there was a trunk full of treasure. Just sitting there!

"Sadly, only a few of her things have been found," Mr. Vorpal went on. "A silk handkerchief. A deck of cards. And this strange object."

He pulled out a small, bent wooden cap, about as long as a thumb.

"A thumb cover!" Max said. "I know how that works. It's a great trick. First you ask for money, then stuff it in your fist. But you're really wearing a fake thumb. So you hide the money under it and —"

"Ssshh!" Quincy put his hand over Max's mouth. "You're giving away our trick!"

Mr. Snodgrass, one of the teachers, was pulling papers out of a briefcase. "Let's not waste time. Children, you must choose your activity for the weekend — Outdoor Survival, Extreme Sports, or Cosmic Crafts. Here are the sign-up sheets."

As the kids rushed forward, Jessica pulled Selena, Max, and Quincy aside. "Looks like we have a new mystery," she said excitedly.

"The missing Vorpal fortune," Quincy added. "A real treasure chest!"

"We'll be rich!" said Selena.

At that moment, Mr. Beamish stepped through the front door. He was dragging his big old trunk. "*Ladieeees and gentlemen!* I shall perform a trick to amaze the senses! More spectacular than a puff of smoke! More wonderful than a dove up a sleeve! It's the Incredible Disappearing Trunk!"

"Oh, dear," moaned Mr. Snodgrass.

"Hmmm . . ." said Mr. Vorpal.

Mr. Beamish set the trunk down, just inside the door. As everyone gathered around, he opened it. "Totally empty, see? Now watch." He took Quincy's notepad and dropped it inside. "I say the magic spell, *Vorpal Vorpalis* — and look!"

He opened the trunk and tilted it forward again. The notepad was gone.

"But — my maps!" Quincy said.

"Cool!" shouted Andrew Flingus. "Make *me* disappear!"

"Great idea," said Selena.

"Do it!" shouted one of the fourth-grade girls.

Mr. Beamish scratched his head. "I've never done this trick with a person. . . ."

"Go! Go! Go! Go!" everyone shouted.

"Okay," Mr. Beamish said with a shrug. "Get in and crouch down, Andrew."

Andrew stepped into the trunk. He was eating a Yankee Doodle. He crammed the last part of it into his mouth. Then he put his hand on his heart and knelt. "Farewell, my friends! Don't cry too much. HAR! HAR! HAR!"

Mr. Beamish quickly closed the top. "And now . . . *Vorpal vorpalis*!"

He tilted the trunk forward. He opened the lid. Andrew had disappeared!

Selena smiled. "Hooray!"

"Come now, we'll miss the old fellow," Mr. Beamish said, closing the top and tilting the trunk back down. "Let's make him appear again! *Vorpalis vorpal!*"

He opened the trunk. As he looked inside, his face went pale.

Only one thing was inside. Quincy's notepad. Covered with Yankee Doodle stains.

Andrew was really, truly gone.

3

Trail of Trash

"Oh, dear," said Mr. Vorpal. "Oh, dear, dear . . ."

"I don't understand," said Mr. Beamish, examining the trunk. "It was just a harmless trick. . . ."

Selena went behind the trunk. The door to the next room was open a bit. It was wide enough for someone to crawl through. "He could have snuck out here."

"I'm sure he's just hiding," Mr. Beamish said. "Selena, Jessica, Max, and Quincy — we'll check outside. The rest of you split up and search the lodge."

Selena and Jessica ran to their room and got their coats. They joined Max, Quincy, and Mr. Beamish outside by the pool. They looked in the ski equipment shed. They checked the grill. But Andrew was nowhere to be found.

Mr. Beamish wiped his brow and gazed up the mountain behind the lodge. "Do you think he went up there?"

"Andrew doesn't even like to climb stairs," said Selena.

"Unless there's food at the top," Jessica added.

"Let's check the kitchen!" Quincy said.

They raced around to the back of the lodge. Through a screen door, Selena could smell roast chicken.

A stack of boxes had been piled near the screen door. A delivery truck was pulling away. The words FROST VILLAGE SWEET SHOP were printed across the side.

Quincy raced to the boxes. He picked up a crumpled candy wrapper. "Snickers," he said.

By the edge of the woods, Selena saw a bit of silver foil. "Twix!"

A narrow path led into the woods. Mr. Beamish signaled the others to follow him. A few feet ahead, a Three Musketeers wrapper was stuck in a tree. Just beyond that, ants were munching on a piece of pretzel. And not much farther, two small birds were fighting over a chunk of potato chip.

"Oh, Andrew?" Quincy called out. "Come out, come out, wherever you are!"

They followed the wrappers. The path twisted, forked, and forked again.

"That boy sure has some appetite," Mr. Beamish said.

Then, as they reached a small crossing, the wrapper trail ended.

A marker stood at the crossing. It was made from a dead tree trunk, and in the afternoon shadows it looked like a bent old witch. Nailed to it were wooden planks that pointed to different places: THE CROSS-EYED NEWT, THE BENT THUMB, THE SINGING NOSTRIL.

"I say we head for the Nostril," Max said. "Andrew would pick that one."

"I say w-w-we head home," said Selena.

Quincy walked around the tree. One of the planks in back was covered tightly with vines. He dug his fingers in and pulled.

The vines were tough, but he ripped them away one by one. Slowly, the plank began to swing out. "It's on a hinge!" he said. "Help me out!"

The Cross-Eyed Newt
The Singing Nostril
The Bent Thumb

Selena joined him, then Jessica and Max. As they tore away the last vines, the plank swung more. It revealed a door that opened into the trunk. The door was small and square, just big enough to reach into.

"Well, uh — who's going to reach inside?" Selena said. "I would, but I, um, I just had my nails done and —"

Jessica let out a deep breath and stuck her hand right in.

She pulled out a mass of twigs, string, and dirt. When she shook all the junk loose, a yellow envelope remained. On it, written in black ink, were some faded letters.

O PAL FORT NE

"What does *that* mean?" Selena asked.

Max tapped his chin. "Looks like elf language to me. . . ."

"NE could mean northeast," said Mr. Beamish.

Jessica held the envelope closer. "There's faded ink between some of the letters. *Fort ne* could be one word."

"Fortane, fortine . . ." Quincy mumbled. "*Fortune!* The word is *fortune*!" He took out his notepad and began writing fast.

"O Pal Fortune?" Selena asked.

"I know!" said Max. "It's *troll* language!"

Quincy dropped his notepad. His mouth was wide open. "Not 'O Pal' — *Vorpal*!"

"Th-th-the V-Vorpal fortune?" said Selena, feeling suddenly weak. "In that envelope?"

"Maybe it's a check for a zillion dollars!" Max said.

"Oh!" gasped Selena. "Oh, my goodness. I — I have to sit down."

Jessica ripped open the envelope. Inside was a yellow, crumbling sheet of paper. And on it was a strange note.

He who knows where it is must go now - Finster!
The money is gone, and oh, is it missed!
Into a fist, with a pat and a twist

4

The Envelope, Please

Max nodded. "*Definitely* troll language."

"Will you stop it?" Selena said. "This is a clue! If we can solve it, we'll all be rich!"

"Uh, guys?" Mr. Beamish said, looking at his watch. "Aren't we forgetting something?"

"Dinner?" Max asked.

Brrrrup! came a noise from the woods.

"Andrew!" they all cried out at the same time.

Jessica yanked aside the branches of a thick bush. Andrew was lying in the grass. He had chocolate stains on his cheeks and an orange ring of Chee-tos dust around his mouth. "Too much food . . ." he moaned. "It's not my fault. All I wanted to do was help those candy guys in the truck, and —"

"Andrew Flingus," Jessica said angrily, her hands on her hips, "it is getting dark, we are deep in the woods, everyone is worried about us, and you're . . . you're . . ."

"You're welcome," Andrew grunted.

"Huh?" said Jessica.

"You should be thanking me. I helped you find the Vorpal fortune, didn't I?" Andrew asked. "I heard what you just found."

"Well, we haven't found it yet," Mr. Beamish said. "And Jessica's right. We must

get back before it's dark. We can search for the treasure tomorrow."

Jessica was angry, but she knew Mr. Beamish was right. She quickly led the way back.

Mr. Beamish made Andrew pick up all his trash as they went. To Selena, it didn't seem like trash anymore. The silver candy wrappers, the golden butterscotch candies, the round, white yogurt balls — they all reminded her of gold, silver, pearls, and coins. All the treasure that would soon be hers!

When they finally reached the lodge, kids and teachers ran out to greet them. "One at a time!" Andrew said, finally feeling stronger. "Autographs are one dollar each! Har! Har! Har!"

"Ah, they found you!" Mr. Vorpal put his arm around Andrew and walked him into the lodge. "You must be frightened and hungry. You need your strength. Our chef will fix you up with carrot juice and wonderful turnip-and-cheese soup. . . ."

Andrew's face slowly began to turn green.

"Come on," Quincy whispered. "Let's solve this clue before dinner!"

Selena, Jessica, Max, and Quincy ran through the lodge and into Quincy's room. They put the secret message on the dresser.

Max studied it carefully. "We need some woodland woo-woo dust."

"What?" said Selena.

"You get it from fairies, I think," Max replied. "Just sprinkle it on, and the message becomes clear."

"It looks like Russian," said Jessica.

"It looks like code," said Quincy.

"It looks like straw!" Selena cried out, staring at her hair in Quincy's mirror. It was all tangled. She took a brush from her backpack and began pulling it through her hair. "We'd better get that message right. Because I am not going to spend a long time in those woods again. Look at these split ends!"

"Selena," Quincy said, looking up, "if you would spend less time in front of a mirror and more time —"

He stopped. His eyes fixed on something in the mirror. He looked at the message that he was holding in his hands. Then he looked up again.

Jumping up from the desk, he stood next to Selena. He turned the message upside down. Then he held it in front of the glass.

Into a fist, with a pat and a twist,
The money is gone, and oh, is it missed!
He who knows where it is must go now - I insist!

"You did it, Quincy! You're a mad genius!" Max began dancing around the room, his cape flying. Then he stopped. "Uh, wait. What does it mean?"

"It's a clue!" Quincy said. "We have to figure it out! The money . . . that must mean the fortune . . ."

"Gone . . . into a fist," Jessica said. "Sounds like a magic trick."

"The treasure disappeared into a fist?" Selena said.

Max took a five-dollar bill from his pocket. He folded it up into a thin rectangle.

"I SHALL NOW MAKE THIS BILL VANISH BY SAYING THE MAGIC WORDS ABRACADABRA . . . ZOT . . . BEEBLE!"

Max made a fist with his left hand and shoved the bill into it. Then he opened his fist . . . and the five-dollar bill was gone.

Jessica reached out and grabbed Max's right thumb. She pulled off a bent plastic thumb covering, and the five-dollar bill fell out. "The old plastic thumb trick!"

Max nodded. "Velma Vorpal's trick!"

"Thumb . . . thumb . . ." Quincy said. "Wait a minute. Those signs on the trail marker — what did they say?"

"The Stinking Nostril . . ." Max said.

"*Singing*," Jessica corrected him. "And the Cross-eyed Newt . . ."

"And the *Bent Thumb*!" Quincy said. "That must be where the treasure is!"

"Where's the Bent Thumb?" Selena asked.

"I don't know," Quincy said, pulling his Frost Village map out of his front pocket, "but we're going there tomorrow."

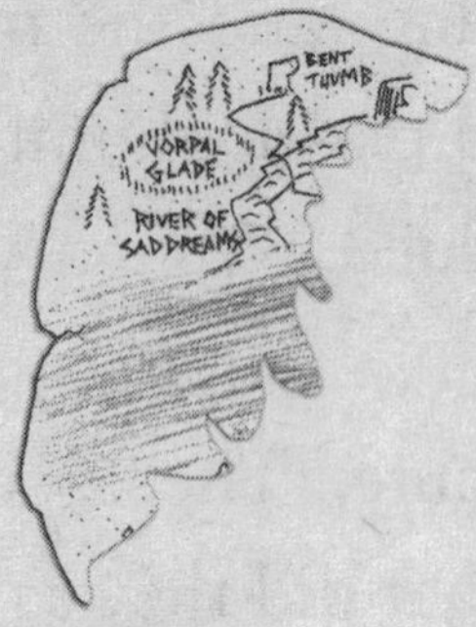

5

Cable Vision

"What do you mean, you want to find the treasure?" Mr. Vorpal asked at the end of breakfast the next morning. "Do you know how many people have already tried? Dozens. Maybe hundreds."

"I know we can do it," Quincy replied, picking up his backpack. "We're the Abracadabra Club. Mystery is our middle name."

"I'll bring my book of magic spells," Max added. "In case of an emergency."

"Just think, Mr. Vorpal," Jessica said, "we will be hiking through the woods. We'll be climbing up mountains. So this is a great Outdoor Survival activity."

"Please?" said Selena. She couldn't believe she was begging to spend a day in the woods.

"The Extreme Sports group will be doing archery, water polo, and softball," Mr. Vorpal said. "The Cosmic Crafts kids will be working with wood and making pots. Don't you want to do those things?"

No one nodded yes.

"We want to find the hidden fortune," Quincy said. "Not only for us, but for Frost Village, for Velma — and for you, Mr. Vorpal."

"What do you say, Victor?" asked Mr. Beamish. "It's okay with me."

Mr. Vorpal took a deep breath. "Well, when you put it like that . . ."

"Thank you!" shouted Selena and Jessica, throwing their arms around him.

"Thank you!" yelled Andrew Flingus from behind them. "HAR! HAR! HAR!"

Max turned around. "Who invited you?"

"Hey, I was the one who led you to the secret clue!" Andrew replied.

"You didn't *lead* us," Jessica said.

"Did too!" Andrew said. "Didn't I, Mr. Beamish?"

"Andrew, what you did yesterday was wrong," Mr. Beamish said. "But I guess if it weren't for you, we wouldn't be doing this. So you can come along."

Andrew grinned.

"I can't believe this," Selena said as she

picked up her backpack from a corner of the cafeteria. "He smells like rotten bananas."

"Be strong," Jessica said. "Think of the Vorpal fortune."

The Abracadabra Club and Andrew walked out of the lodge and into the woods. At the start of a trail, Mr. Beamish pointed to a blue circle painted on a tree trunk. "This mark is called a blaze," he said. "The path to the Bent Thumb is lined with trees that have blue blazes. We must follow them. We will travel in pairs — Jessica and Max first, then Selena and Quincy, followed by Andrew and me. Everyone has packed enough food and water for a long day's hike. Try not to eat or drink too much at the start, or you'll run out later. Any questions?"

"Yeah." Andrew raised his hand. "When's lunch?"

Selena didn't wait to hear the answer.

She marched down the trail with Quincy. As Andrew began walking with Mr. Beamish, he unwrapped a Mars bar. "For energy," he explained.

As the group went deeper into the woods, the sounds of Frost Village faded. For a long, long time no one said a word. Birds sang sweetly in the sunlight. Footsteps crunched on the pathway. Food crunched in Andrew's mouth.

Soon Andrew's eating made Selena feel hungry. She began eating some of her food. So did Jessica and Quincy. And Max and Mr. Beamish.

"Acka way hoo fada fezzer," said Andrew.

"Swallow, please," said Selena.

Andrew gulped. "I can't wait to find the treasure! I'll even share some with you guys."

"*Some?*" Selena said. "You're going to have to pull the jewelry out of my hands, Andrew."

"Yuck. I hate jewelry," Andrew said.

"I want to read Velma's magic books," Quincy said. "Mr. Vorpal said they were made before printing was invented. Monks wrote the words out by hand."

"I didn't know animals could write back then," said Andrew.

"Not monkeys," Quincy replied. "*Monks!*"

A rushing noise began to drown out their voices. Just around the next bend, Jessica and Max had stopped short.

They were on the bank of a river. It was too wide to cross by foot. The water flowed fast, splashing against big white rocks.

Not too far away, three metal cables stretched across the river. The cables were tied at each end to tree trunks. It looked like a bridge — one cable for feet, the other two a bit higher for handrails. The cables were tied to each other with thin wires.

On the other side of the river was a tree with a blue blaze.

"Uh-oh," said Selena. "Looks like our trail crosses the river."

"Let's walk along the river until we find a narrow spot," said Mr. Beamish.

"But that may take too long," Quincy said. "We'll lose the trail."

"The cable looks like it'll hold our weight," Jessica said.

Max pulled a funny-looking card from a pocket in his cape. "This is a special magic forest card. It has Flying, and a strength of plus-five. Take it and you cannot fall."

"Max, will you *stop* it with the silly spells?" Selena said.

"Well," Mr. Beamish said, grabbing onto a tree branch, "I guess if the cables can hold me, they'll hold you." Carefully he climbed the tree. He stepped onto the bottom cable. He draped his arms over the two higher ones. As he took a step, the cable sagged. It shook and wobbled. Mr. Beamish's face was quickly covered with sweat.

Selena held her breath. This was crazy. Totally crazy. She waited for him to turn around and come back.

But he didn't. He kept going — and when he reached the other side, he jumped off. "Hey, that was fun!" he said with a grin. "Selena, you try!"

"Oh, no," said Selena. "No, no, no. Not in a million, billion, gazillion years."

"Help me up then," said Jessica. "We'll share the treasure without you."

Selena took a deep breath. "Max? Give me that card!"

She took the magic card from Max and climbed the tree. Her legs felt weak. Her head spun. The bridge was rocking in the wind. With shaking hands she grabbed onto the cables. Slowly, she stepped out.

Don't look down, she said to herself. *Don't look down.*

"Under your armpits!" Mr. Beamish called out. "Keep the two higher cables under your —"

The cable wobbled right. It wobbled left.

Selena looked down.

Suddenly, her foot slipped. She let out a scream. And she fell.

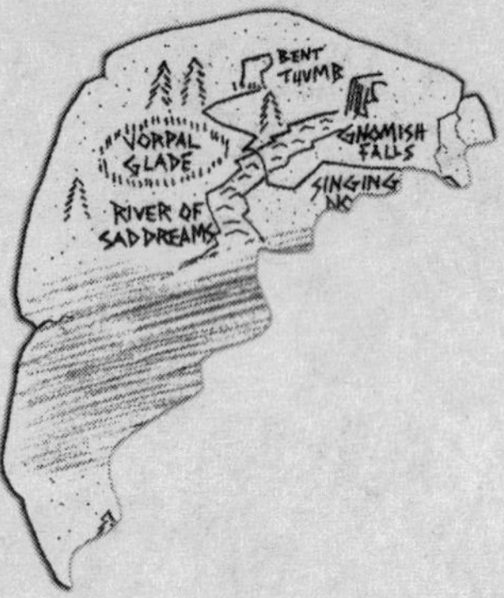

6

Outdoor Survival

"AAAAAAGH!"

Selena was dangling. The upper cables had caught her under the arms. But her feet were swinging over the water. She felt the water rushing up from below. Her heart was pounding like a small animal trying to escape. She tried to yell, but no sound would come out.

"Hold on, Selena!" Jessica shouted. "Just lift your feet onto the cable!"

"I can't watch this," Quincy said, turning away in terror. He couldn't see anyway because his glasses were all dirty and crooked.

Selena placed her feet on the bottom cable. Slowly, she stood. The rushing water splashed up from below. She inched forward. The cables shook with every step, but she held on tight.

When she came close enough, Mr. Beamish pulled her onto the bank. "Are you okay?" he asked.

"N-next time, I'm doing C-c-cosmic Crafts," Selena said, sinking to the ground.

One by one, the others came across. They all stood at the head of the blue blaze path. Selena joined them, her knees shaking. From this side of the river, they could see where the blue blaze path led — to a steep mountain trail of white rocks.

"Maybe we should go back," Selena said.

"If we could handle that bridge," Jessica said, "we can handle anything."

A deep sound came up from the river. *RRRRUMMMMMMM!*

"Yeeps!" squeaked Quincy.

"I lied," said Jessica. "RUN!"

She sped into the woods with Selena, Quincy, and Max behind her.

"AAAAGHHHHH!" came Andrew's voice. "It got me! *It got my foot!*"

Selena spun around. "Andrew — are you all right?"

Andrew was still near the river. His foot was caught in a root. "Made you look! Made you look! HAR! HAR! HAR!"

"But — ?" Selena said. "But what was — ?"

Mr. Beamish came running up the path

from the river. “A big, bad bullfrog!” he called out.

“I — I knew that,” Quincy said calmly.

“I hate the outdoors,” Selena said to Jessica. “I hate hate *hate* the outdoors.”

Jessica reached the white rocks first. She started to climb. They were covered with thick dust, which made Quincy sneeze. Max’s wet sneakers slipped as he climbed. He had to keep ducking, because Jessica was knocking rocks down from above.

At the top, Selena’s fingers were raw. Her legs ached and her hair was dusty. Even worse, her jeans were filthy and her designer jacket was ripped.

They had climbed to the edge of a field. In the middle of it was a tall rock with weeds all around it. It was crooked and narrow, rising straight up out of the ground and then off to an angle. Like a finger. Or . . .

"*The Bent Thumb!*" Andrew screamed, running toward the rock. "I said it first! It's my treasure! HAR! HAR! HAR!"

"That's not fair!" Quincy said, chasing after him.

Soon they were all poking around the rock, kicking the dirt. The treasure had to be around there somewhere. Andrew climbed the rock, beating away branches with his backpack.

Suddenly, with a loud *SHHHUNK*, the tip of the rock slid to the side.

"Oops," said Andrew, jumping off. "Guess I don't know my own strength."

Quincy gave the tip a push, and it moved farther. It was broken clean across, in a perfectly straight line. "It's not *natural* for a rock to be broken so smoothly. This rock was cut by a saw or a machine."

"They had machines in the sixteen-hundreds?" Selena asked.

Quincy slid the rest of the tip of the rock off. With a heavy thump, it fell into the grass. Under it, the bottom section of the rock was flat and smooth.

Something was carved into it — a treasure map.

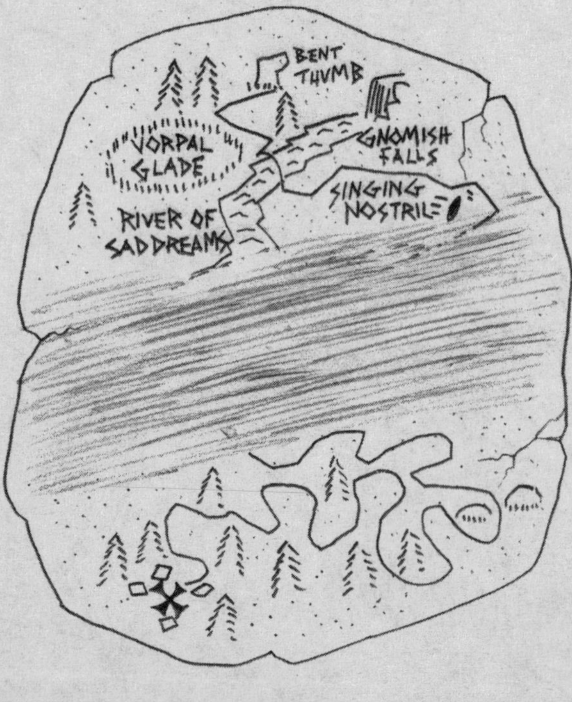

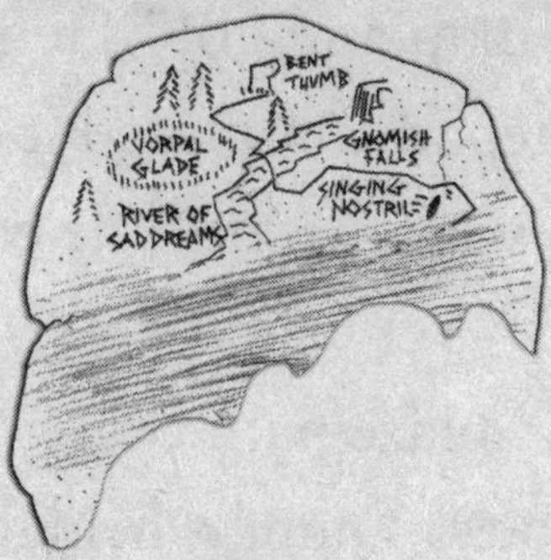

7

It's in the Cards

"What's that shape at the end?" Jessica asked.

"Looks like a skull," Max said. "X marks the spot."

"But how do we get there?" Selena remarked. "There's no middle section to the map!"

"We should be okay if we follow the blue blazes," Quincy said. "Let's make a copy of the map and go!" He ripped a page from his notepad and placed it on the carved rock. Then, with a pencil, he carefully made a tracing.

The blue blaze path began again just beyond the rock. Quincy held out the map, leading the way. When the path curved, the line on the map curved. When it went straight, the path on the map did the same.

The sun was directly overhead now. It made speckles of light on the forest floor. The cool day had turned very warm.

After a long while they reached a clearing. "This isn't on the map," Quincy said. "We've reached the missing part of the map."

Selena looked around. "No more blue blazes, either."

They walked into the sunlight. In the middle of the clearing was a low stone wall. It made a square shape, as if it had once been a small house. A junk pile was in the center — burnt wood, garbage, and more stones. Everything was covered with grass and weeds.

Selena stood on the wall and looked around. At the other side of the clearing, four paths led into the woods. Each was marked with a different blaze — a yellow square, a purple line, a red diamond shape, and a white X.

"Now what?" Andrew asked.

"I don't know," Quincy said.

"Let's just pick one path," Selena declared. "Eenie, meenie, miney, mo . . ."

"Not so fast," Mr. Beamish said. He was climbing over the wall, looking at the stones. "This is a great example of early New England house construction."

"Early *what*?" said Jessica.

"I'm hungry," Andrew complained.

Mr. Beamish began picking things out of the junk pile. Selena saw something shine in the sun's rays.

Something gold.

"Look!" she cried out, jumping over the stone wall. Digging in, she pulled a small box out of the vines and dirt.

"Is that *it*?" Jessica asked. "Is that the treasure?"

Selena shook the box. It was made of brass or gold. Something rattled inside. She grabbed the latch and pulled the top open.

"Empty," Max said.

"I don't think so," Selena said. She held the box up to the light. She could see a thin line, running around the whole box.

The little box had a fake bottom. She grabbed it and pulled. Slowly, a small, flat section slid out. In the middle was a folded-up playing card. It was decorated with a fancy V V.

"Velma Vorpal . . ." Quincy said.

Selena turned the card over. On the other side was a rhyme:

> **WHEN UPSIDE DOWN, A THING CAN BE**
> **NOT AT ALL WHAT FIRST YOU SEE!**
> **SO, TOO, ABOVE THE QUEEN AND KING,**
> **ONE HEART BECOMES ANOTHER THING.**

"Big help," Selena said with a sigh.

"Poetry," groaned Andrew. "Yuck."

"Now, wait," Mr. Beamish said. "Maybe it's a clue. 'So, too, above the queen and king . . .'"

"No one is above the king and queen," Jessica replied, "except in a deck of cards."

"Yes! The *ace* is higher than both of them!" Quincy said, grabbing the poem from Selena. "What's the next part? 'One heart becomes another thing . . .'"

"Heart!" Max blurted out. "The ace of hearts!"

"Okay," Jessica said, "so we know the ace of hearts 'becomes another thing' . . . 'when upside down. . . .'"

Quincy was deep in thought. "Let me try something . . ."

He reached into his backpack and took out a deck of cards. He always carried it in case of a magic emergency. He took out one

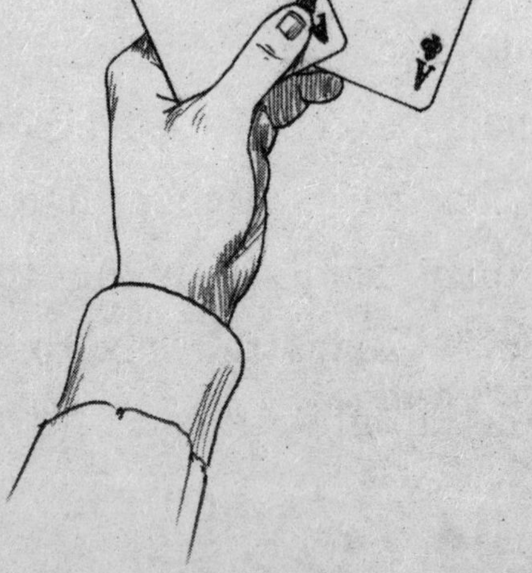

card — then another and another. He held them out for everyone to see.

"Okay, everybody," Quincy said. "Name the card in the middle!"

"Ace of Diamonds," Mr. Beamish replied.

Quincy pulled away the other cards. "Abracadabra!"

"'One heart becomes another thing'!" Jessica said. "The heart became a diamond!"

"Which means," Quincy said with a grin, "we follow the diamond blaze trail. That will lead us to the treasure!"

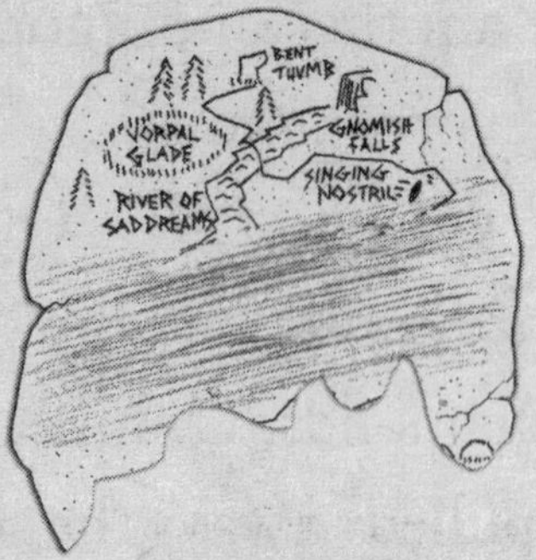

8

Diamond Dig

Quincy wiped his forehead. He laid the map on a flat rock.

"Are we there yet?" Andrew whined.

"Almost," said Quincy.

Selena stopped to catch her breath. They were past the missing section of the map now. They had guessed the clue correctly. The red diamond path was following all the curves on the map. But it was long and narrow. They had been walking over boulders and wading through streams. And they were all tired.

"I can just taste the treasure," Selena said.

"I can just taste a Snickers bar," Andrew added.

Thwock!

Selena jumped to her feet. The sound came from around the corner. It was far off, but everyone heard it.

"Sounds like an ax," Jessica said.

"Or a party of giants bowling with pine trees!" Max exclaimed.

Quincy grabbed the map. "Someone must be there already. Let's go!"

They ran down the path. Selena passed Max, Quincy, Jessica, and Mr. Beamish. Her feet caught on rocks. Branches whipped against her face. Soon she came to a field —

a big field with beautiful green grass. They had reached the map's end.

"Selena? Is that you?"

Selena turned. The voice belonged to Erica Landers, a girl from school. She was standing in a field just ahead and wearing a baseball cap. Behind her was another classmate. And another.

And beyond them, two teams of classmates were playing softball.

"Of course!" Jessica exclaimed, running up beside Selena. "The shape at the end of the map — it's a baseball diamond!"

"Softball," Erica corrected her. "Extreme softball."

"The secret treasure is hidden under the X on this map!" Quincy said, holding out the map.

Jessica looked at the drawing curiously. "The pitcher's mound?"

"Get a shovel!" Quincy yelled, running across the field. "*Someone get a shovel!*"

Mr. Vorpal had lots of shovels, and he handed them all out. He even helped with the digging himself. He looked very excited.

Selena dug until her nail polish was scraped off. When they got four inches down, they heard a *thunk*. Everyone dug some more, until the outline of something appeared.

Something big and made of black wood, with gold metal bands all around it.

Selena couldn't stop smiling. Her blood raced.

The sun was beginning to set as they finally pulled the trunk out of the ground. It was huge and old and heavy.

"We did it!" shouted Quincy. "*We solved the mystery!*"

"I'll be able to buy a new bike," Jessica said.

"I won't have to shop only on sale days!" Selena exclaimed.

"I'm so excited, I'm not even hungry!" Andrew said. "HAR! HAR! HAR!"

Mr. Vorpal stared at the trunk. "The Vorpal fortune . . . after all these years."

"You should be the one to open it," Mr. Beamish said.

"No," said Mr. Vorpal. "Quincy is the one who found it. He can open it."

Quincy swallowed hard. He reached out to the handle and gripped it tightly. Then he slowly lifted the lid.

9

Vorpal Vorpalis

A spider crawled out. A bug curled up into a ball on the floor of the trunk.

And that was it. Nothing else.

The trunk was totally empty.

“It can’t be,” said Selena.

Quincy slowly closed the trunk. “Robbers must have gotten it.”

Selena sat on a bench. Her whole body

hurt. As the softball teams went back onto the field, tears began to run down her cheeks.

"It's okay," Jessica said gently.

But it wasn't okay. It was all for nothing. Everything. The whole trip.

"Well, you all solved a mystery that no one else has," Mr. Vorpal said. "I'm sure Velma would be proud of you — and I am, too. Now, come, why don't we go back, and I'll cheer you up with a new magic trick. I can make myself vanish inside a model of the Vorpal lodge."

Mr. Beamish yawned. "That's old. I'll bring a *real* trick from my room."

As Mr. Beamish ran ahead, Mr. Vorpal chuckled. "Always trying to compete. You know, your teacher is a fine magician. But he really should take a few lessons from me."

He began walking down a path toward

the lodge. Selena, Quincy, Jessica, and Max walked behind him, not saying a word.

Mr. Vorpal led them into a room off the main lobby. It had a few seats and a small stage. "This is where I put on my shows," he said, pulling back a curtain.

At the center of the stage were four folded-up walls and a roof. They were parts of a model of the Vorpal lodge. The roof was on its side and the walls were leaning against it. They were about as high as Mr. Vorpal's waist.

He unfolded one of the walls. It looked real. Then he unfolded the other wall and put it in place. It was a perfect mini-Vorpal lodge, without a roof. "I shall put the roof on, then climb inside," Mr. Vorpal said. "Then you will clap three times, and I will be gone!"

"Cool," said Max.

Mr. Vorpal put the roof on the lodge.

"Now," he said, "I shall give it magical properties . . . by chanting *VORPAL VORPALIS* —"

Suddenly, the roof moved.

Mr. Vorpal gasped and jumped back. "Oh!"

"Yeeps," cried Quincy.

Slowly, the roof rose upward. From underneath came a deep voice: "You need to chant more slowly, Victor — it works better that way."

It was Mr. Beamish!

Selena nearly fell off her seat.

"But — how — ?" Jessica said.

Quincy began to clap. Max joined in.

Mr. Vorpal broke out laughing. So did Mr. Beamish. They put their arms around each other and took a bow.

"Remember," Mr. Beamish said, "sometimes an empty space is not what it seems!"

The words seemed to hit Jessica over the head. She thought about the little box with the message, and Mr. Beamish's trunk that Andrew "vanished" into.

And she thought of the Vorpal fortune in the big, empty trunk.

"We have to go back," she said suddenly, nearly knocking over her chair as she stood. "We have to go back to the baseball field. I know where the fortune is!"

10

Reaching Bottom

Jessica nearly flew down the path, with the others close behind.

The trunk was sitting at the edge of the softball diamond. Andrew was leaning against it. He had a slice of pizza in one hand and an ice-cream cone in the other.

He moved aside as Jessica opened the lid. Reaching inside, she knocked on the bottom.

Pock. Pock. Pock.

"What are you doing?" asked Selena.

"It's hollow," Jessica explained. "There's something else in here. Under a false bottom."

Jessica felt the thick metal strips on the trunk's sides. They were carved into fancy designs. She pulled at the edges until something clicked.

It was a latch. There was one on the left and one on the right. She snapped them both open.

The top half of the trunk swung away. Under it was another section. It was just as big as the other half.

And it was full. Quincy lifted out a heavy book with the words ANCIENT MAGICK ARTS written in gold lettering. "It's beautiful," he said.

Folded beneath the book was a gown made of red silk. Bright rubies were sewn onto the fabric. They glowed as Selena lifted the gown. It was the most wonderful thing she had ever seen.

Max took out a long magic wand, made of polished marble.

Jessica pulled out juggling balls and magic dust. A velvet cape and a flat black hat that popped out into a top hat. Strange ancient playing cards and silken ropes. Fancy mirrors and false fingers.

"My, my . . ." Mr. Vorpal said. "I never thought I'd see this again."

"Again?" Quincy asked.

"Did I say that?" Mr. Vorpal said with a giggle. "I meant, I thought I'd never see it at all."

"What will you do with it?" Mr. Beamish asked.

"That's a good question," Mr. Vorpal said. "I can't really keep it here. And I

wouldn't sell it. Perhaps a museum would want it."

"You know," Jessica said, "the Abracadabra Club would take great care of it."

Mr. Vorpal stroked his beard. He looked out over the field. Max was whooshing the velvet cape through the air. Quincy was reading the old book. Selena was holding the gown against her.

"Beamish," Mr. Vorpal finally said, "do you have room for the Vorpal fortune on your bus back to Rebus?"

Mr. Beamish nodded. "We could find room."

"Then — *Vorpal Vorpalis* — it's yours!" Mr. Vorpal said.

Selena screamed with happiness. She, Jessica, Max, and Quincy rushed to Mr. Vorpal at the same time.

As they all fell to the ground, laughing,

Andrew peeked inside the trunk. Pizza sauce and chocolate ice cream dripped from the corners of his mouth. "It's just magic stuff," he said. "No money."

Selena brushed herself off and stood up. "This is better than money."

"The finest magic treasure in the world," said Mr. Vorpal, smiling proudly. "Did you find the silk ropes?"

Max ran to the trunk and lifted them out. "Here they are!"

Quincy gave Mr. Vorpal a funny look. "Wait. How did you know about them?"

Mr. Vorpal's smile vanished. "Well — Velma *had* to have silk ropes. Most magicians did, back then. Isn't that right, Beamish?"

"Uh, yes," Mr. Beamish said. "Right."

Jessica stood slowly, folding her arms.

"Wait a minute. Did you two *know* this treasure was here?"

Mr. Vorpal and Mr. Beamish both looked shocked. "*Us?*" they said together.

Jessica thought back. Some parts of the trip still seemed strange. Like the time Mr. Beamish just *happened* to find the brass box. And the way Mr. Vorpal knew about the silk ropes. And the way the paths on an ancient treasure map were *exactly* the same as the paths now. With exactly the same blaze. With a baseball field in *exactly* the same place.

"Mr. Beamish . . . ?" Jessica said. "Was there baseball in the 1600s?"

Her teacher laughed. "Of course not."

"Then that means . . ."

Jessica stopped in the middle of her sentence. No one else was listening. They were all gathered around the chest. Smiling and laughing. Pulling out the most amazing tricks and magical objects.

All Jessica wanted to do was join them. She knelt down and reached into the chest.

"That means what?" Mr. Beamish asked.

"Never mind," Jessica said.

Some questions, she decided, would just have to wait.

The Abracadabra Files by Quincy

Magic Trick #7

The Disappearing Trunk

Ingredients:
Special trunk, made with a fake bottom (see drawing):

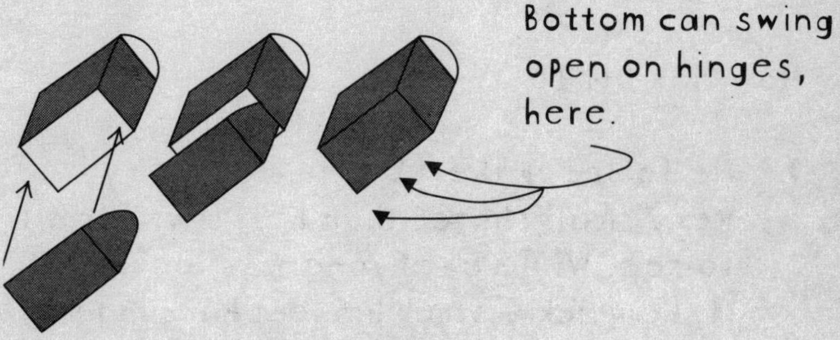
Bottom can swing open on hinges, here.

How Mr. Beamish Did It:

When Mr. Beamish tilted the trunk forward, the bottom part swung outward. Andrew was hidden inside. He could easily slip away!

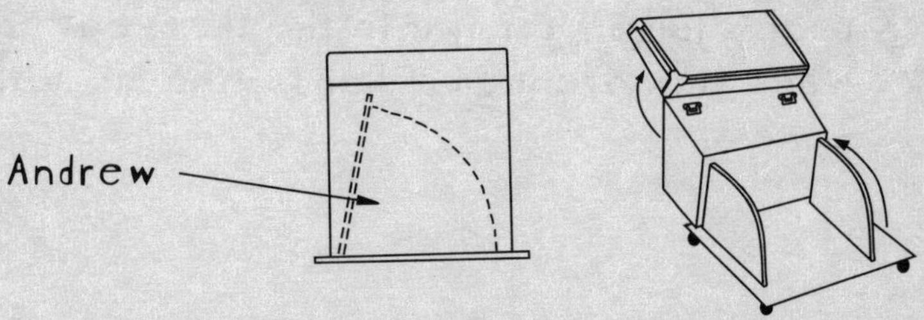
Andrew

<u>The Abracadabra Files</u> by Quincy

Magic Trick #8

The Bent Thumb/Disappearing Bill Trick

Ingredients:
one bill of money ($1, $5, $10, etc.)
one plastic, skin-colored thumb cover

How Max Did It:

1. He folded up the $5 bill into a very, very small shape, then held it up for all to see. While everyone was looking at it, he quickly stuck his left hand in his pocket. The plastic thumb cover was there. He slipped his thumb into it.
2. When he took out his left hand and made a fist, no one noticed he was wearing the thumb cover. They were too busy watching the $5 bill.
3. As he stuffed the bill into his fist, he was really jamming it up into the thumb cover.
4. When Max opened his hands, the bill was gone!

The Abracadabra Files by Quincy

Magic Trick #9

Making an Ace of Diamonds Turn into an Ace of Hearts

Ingredients:
Three Aces — Spades, Clubs, Hearts

How I Did It:

I arranged the cards in my hand so that the ace of hearts was

- behind the others
- upside down, with the bottom tip of the heart facing upward, and

– with the other two cards slanted across the ace in a V-shape, so that the edges of the cards covered all but the heart's tip – which made the heart look like a diamond!

The Abracadabra Files by Quincy

Magic Trick #10

Making Mr. Beamish Appear in the Model of the Vorpal Lodge

Ingredients:
Three parts of a mini house, placed like this:

Roof is put on its side. It doesn't fold.

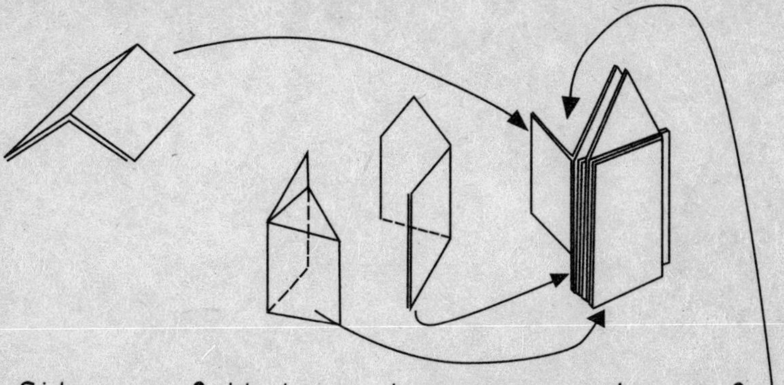

Sides are folded up and put next to the roof.

Mr. Beamish was hiding behind here!

How Mr. Vorpal Did It:

He carefully unfolded the sides into shape, right next to the roof. He didn't allow any space between the roof and the unfolded sides. Mr. Beamish could sneak into the "house."

Mr. B's path

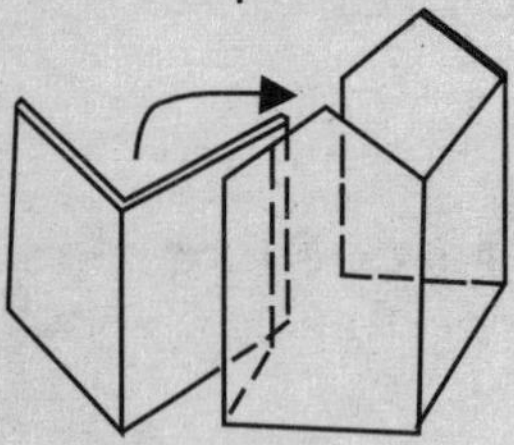

About the Author

Peter Lerangis is the author of many different kinds of books for many ages, including *Watchers*, an award-winning science-fiction/mystery series; *Antarctica*, a two-book exploration adventure; and several hilarious novels for young readers, including *Spring Fever!*, *Spring Break*, *It Came from the Cafeteria*, and *Attack of the Killer Potatoes*. His recent movie adaptations include *The Sixth Sense* and *El Dorado*. He lives in New York City with his wife, Tina deVaron, and their two sons, Nick and Joe.

Coming Soon:

Abracadabra!

Yeeps!

Secret in the Statue!

ATTENTION, ABRACADABRA CLUB!" yelled Jessica Frimmel. "LISTEN UP! I HAVE IMPORTANT NEWS TODAY!"

When Jessica spoke like that, people listened (and sometimes covered their ears). But not that day.

That day was the great opening of the Vorpal treasure chest. The chest had been given to them by a magician named Mr. Vorpal, and it was full of amazing stuff.

Selena Cruz danced by in a long dress. She passed a red feather under Jessica's nose. "Did you say order, daaarling Jessica?" she said with a silly accent. "I order a brand-new diamond ring!"

"Your wish is my command!" shouted Max Bleeker, waving a white marble wand that he'd found in the chest. Max's wand nearly poked Quincy Norton in the glasses. But Quincy didn't notice. He was pulling something out of the chest. Something heavy and wrapped in yellow paper. Quincy pulled back the yellow paper, and came face-to-face with the club's newest mystery.

A glowing red eye was staring back at him.

"Yeeps!" he cried, leaping back. The object slipped out of the paper and dropped to the table with a thud. It was shiny and solid black, with an eye of solid red jewel. It made a sound like solid metal, but the outside of it looked soft and wrinkled, like real skin. It had the long snout of a crocodile. Its chest was large and furry like a lion's, but from the waist down, it looked like a sitting pig.

It was the strangest, most magical-looking thing Jessica had ever seen.

"Oh, my," said Mr. Beamish, tugging on his pointy little beard. "Oh, my my my."

Selena stopped dancing. "Is it . . . alive?"

Max stopped whooshing his cape. "No, but it looks angry."

Jessica stopped yelling. "How can it be dead and angry at the same time?"

"I believe it's a statue," Quincy said, "but a baffling one." Quincy was the kind of kid who said baffling. No one knew why; he was just like that. He was also the only kid in Rebus Elementary School who brought a white cloth napkin to school every day. He pulled it from his pocket and wrapped it around the statue. As he lifted it, its eye seemed to wink.

"Did you see that?" Max exclaimed.

"It was the light," Jessica said.

Quincy began wiping off the statue, and the black color changed to shiny gold.

Max closed his eyes, touching his fingers to his forehead. "I, MAX THE MAGNIFICENT, SHALL CONTACT THE SPIRIT OF THIS . . . THIS DREADED ANCIENT GOLDEN PIG-LION-O-DILE —"

Jessica grabbed his shoulder and plopped him into a seat. "Sit down."

"It is just a statue — it doesn't have magic powers," Quincy said, giving the statue a shake. "Just as I thought. There's something inside. In ancient times, valuable treasures were always hidden in strange, mythical beasts."

Jessica took the statue. It felt warm and smooth. A thin crack ran from top to bottom, with two tiny hinges. She turned the statue in her hand, looking for a secret button or switch. She turned the angry red eye away from her. It was only a jewel, but it scared her.

Then she saw something she didn't expect. It was a hole, where another eye was supposed to be. Around the hole's edges was a thin metal ring. "Look," she said. "It's some kind of clip!"

Quincy leaned in. "Spring-loaded, I'll bet. You put the eye in. Inside the statue, a spring draws back. Then it snaps back to keep the eye in place."

"Or — it springs back to open the statue!" Jessica exclaimed.

"So if we find the other eye, we can unlock the secret treasure!" Selena cried. "Jessica, you're a genius!"